FRIENDS OF ACPL

TREE for RENT

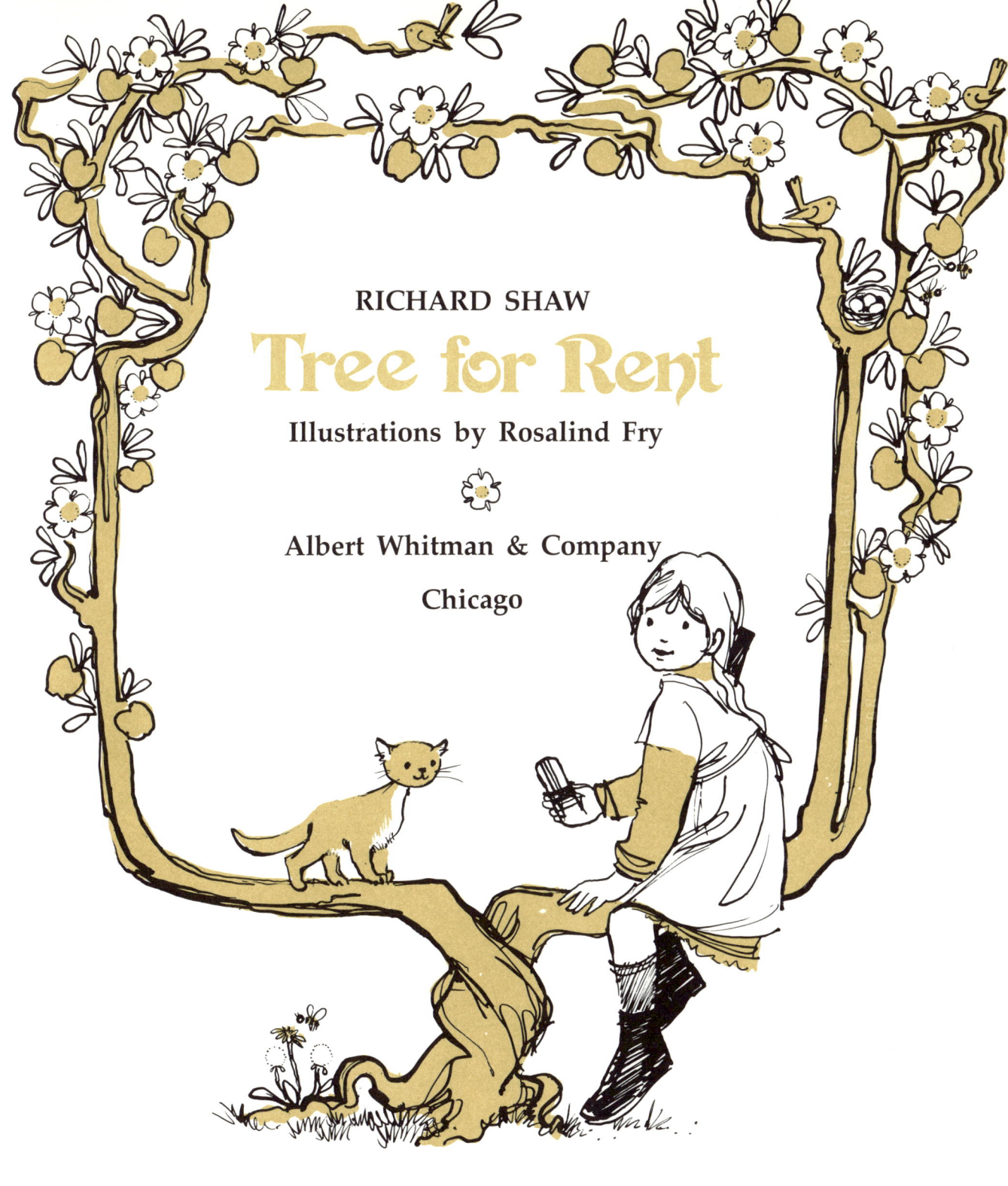

RICHARD SHAW

Tree for Rent

Illustrations by Rosalind Fry

Albert Whitman & Company

Chicago

For Jenny and Her Nana

ISBN 0-8075-8082-1
Library of Congress Card Number 72-165821
Text © Copyright 1971 by Richard Shaw
Illustrations © Copyright 1971 by Rosalind Fry
Published simultaneously in Canada by
George J. McLeod, Limited, Toronto
Lithographed in U.S.A.
All rights reserved

On her way home from school
through the center of town,
Jenny walked very quickly,
then always *ran* down
Maple Street....

...Past the church,
past the store and town hall,
she hurried to Grandma's
to tell Grandma all
of the news of the day—
what she'd seen, whom she'd met.

And while Jenny chattered, her grandma would get out a dish and a glass and some cold lemonade or some chocolate milk or a pie she'd just made.

On a May afternoon,
as she drank lemonade,
Jenny said to her grandma,
"I wonder who made
that hole in the trunk
of the maple? Yes, I'd
just like to know
who is living inside.
Who can it be, Grandma,
living in there?
It could be a possum
or maybe a pair
of squirrels or rabbits
setting up house,
or a couple of chipmunks
or even a mouse."

"We'll just have to watch,"
Grandma said with a smile,
"to see who comes out
or goes in for a while.
I'll ask the postman
when he brings the mail.
And you ask the neighbors,
for certainly they'll
have seen who it is
and most surely would
have heard of new people
in this neighborhood."

After school the next day
Jennifer walked
down the street to her grandma's.
She stopped off and talked
with some men who were loading
a huge moving van,
two men in a ditch,
and the street cleaning man.

She wanted to ask them
whoever could be
setting up house in
the old hollow tree.
But no one could tell her —
yet everyone knew
that somebody lived there.
But not one could say who.

As she raced through the yard,
what Jennifer saw
made her stop by the tree.
"It's a doormat of straw,"
she exclaimed, "with three letters,
two J's and a J."

Jenny ran to the house
calling, "Look, Grandma, they
are people, *real* people,
who live in the tree.
But very small people,
much smaller than me.
Maybe they're goblins.
Just think of that!"
And Jenny showed Grandma
the little straw mat.
"Now who put that mat there
when I wasn't looking?
From my kitchen," said Grandma,
"I watch while I'm cooking.
Tomorrow perhaps
there will be other clues.
Now, come in the kitchen
and tell me the news."

After school the next day Jenny hurried so fast on her way to her grandma's that she nearly ran past. Yes, there by the maple was the mat as before, but the hollow was closed by a tiny green door. Tacked over the door was a very small sign reading "Jingle J. Jones and Wife, Clementine."

"Grandma!" cried Jenny,
"I've found out who owns
the little straw mat.
It's Jingle J. Jones."
"I know some Joneses,"
Grandmother said,
"but they are big Joneses—
Norma, Gladys, and Fred.
Besides, they would never
move into *my* tree
and tack up a sign
without asking me."
"These are *small* Joneses,"
Jenny insisted.
"The smallest small Joneses
that ever existed."

"I'd feel so much better," Grandma said, "if I'd been introduced to the Joneses before they moved in. Well, maybe tomorrow they plan to drop by. Now come in the kitchen. There's warm apple pie."

At her lessons next day
Jenny just couldn't spell.
And adding up numbers
didn't go very well.
She thought about Jingle
and the little green door.
She wrote on her paper
1 + 1 = 4.

"There's the bell!" Jenny ran
through the center of town.
She didn't slow up,
she didn't slow down
till she reached Grandma's yard.
She was eager to see
what might have been changed
at the old hollow tree.
She flopped on her stomach
and peered deep inside,
for the little green door
had been left open wide.
The things Jenny saw
made her blink with surprise—
things Grandma must see
with her very own eyes.

Grandma called from the window,
"Now what have you found?
You'll catch a bad cold —
get up off the ground."
"There's a rug," Jenny cried,
"and a table and chair.
But Jingle and Clementine
are not anywhere."
"A chair and a table?
Hold them up, let me see.
They're just what I'd use
to furnish a tree,"
said Jennifer's grandma
as she came out the door.
"My, that's a fine rug
to cover the floor."

"I wonder," said Jenny,
"where the Joneses can be.
They're not in the yard
and they're not in the tree."

"Both of them probably
spend a full day
at work in the city.
Most likely they
leave the tree very early
and get home rather late,"
Grandma said and then added,
"so we'll just have to wait
till Saturday morning
to pay them a call.
Yes, that will be better.
We'll wait till they're all
settled in. Come along
to the house when you're ready.
I've just finished baking
fresh apple brown betty."

While they sat in the kitchen
Jenny forgot
to eat her brown betty.
"It's best when it's hot,"
said her grandma. "I wonder,"
Jenny replied,
"how long they've been married—
Jingle Jones and his bride.
The table and rug
look as new as the chair.
There are no signs of children
around anywhere.
Do you think Jingle's friendly?
And Clementine pretty?
What can they do
all day long in the city?"

"Maybe Jingle's a painter who paints behind things where big men can't reach.

And Clementine strings the tiniest strands of the shiniest pearls," Grandma guessed, "to make bracelets for pretty young girls."

So certain was Jenny
the following day
she would find something new
that she ran *all* the way
from her school to her grandma's.
She squeezed through the hedge,
and what did she see?
Right close to the edge
of Grandma's herb garden—
not a gnome or an elf,
not a Jones or a goblin—
but Grandma herself!

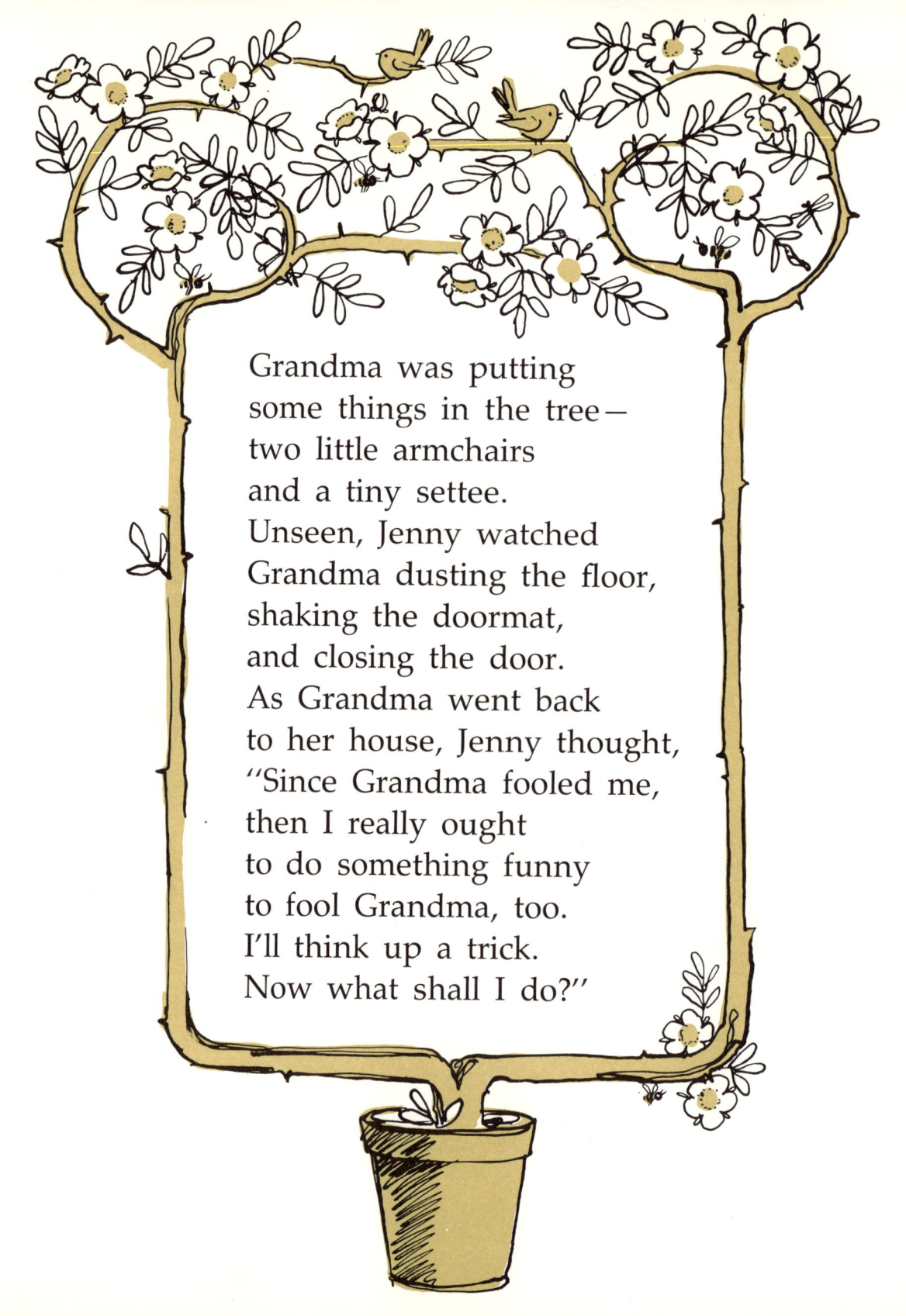

Grandma was putting
some things in the tree—
two little armchairs
and a tiny settee.
Unseen, Jenny watched
Grandma dusting the floor,
shaking the doormat,
and closing the door.
As Grandma went back
to her house, Jenny thought,
"Since Grandma fooled me,
then I really ought
to do something funny
to fool Grandma, too.
I'll think up a trick.
Now what shall I do?"

Jen waited till Grandma
was safely inside,
then raced toward her home
and, not breaking stride,
she bounced up the stairs,
found a paper and pen,
and sat down to write
a letter. And then
holding the letter
she laughed as she ran
back to her grandma's
to finish her plan.

"Grandma, a letter!"
Jennifer cried
as she ran to the kitchen.
"I found it outside."
"A letter? How nice,"
was Grandma's reply.
"But first, is it milk
with your blueberry pie?
There's cake in the breadbox.
Would you like that instead?"
Gran opened the letter
and here's what she read:

*Dear Jenny's Grandma,
Please come to tea.
Bring Jennifer, too.
R.S.V.P.
Saturday morning,
along about nine.
Signed, Jingle J. Jones
and wife, Clementine.*

"How thoughtful," said Grandma,
"of dear Clementine.
But I'm simply too busy—
especially at nine."
"That's funny," said Jenny.
"I'll be busy, too.
It just happens I'll be
at home here with you."
And the very next day
when Jennifer went
to look in the tree,
a sign said: "For Rent."

So the tree game was over.
Jenny felt she might cry
till she heard Grandma call,
"There's Boston cream pie
and devils' food cake.
Which do you choose?
Do come in the kitchen
and tell me the news."